ANIMAL CRACKERS
FLY THE COOP

Kevin O'Malley

Walker & Company New York

For my dad,
who worried we'd grow up with no sense of humor

First published in the United States of America in March 2010 by
Walker Publishing Company, Inc., a division of Bloomsbury Publishing, Inc.
Visit Walker & Company's Web site at www.bloomsburykids.com

For information about permission to reproduce selections from this book, write to
Permissions, Walker & Company, 175 Fifth Avenue, New York, New York 10010

Library of Congress Cataloging-in-Publication Data
O'Malley, Kevin.
Animal crackers fly the coop / Kevin O'Malley. — 1st U.S. ed.
            p.   cm.
Summary: In this humorous take-off of "The Brementown Musicians," four animals
that aspire to make it big as comedians leave their owners and seek their fortunes.
ISBN 978-0-8027-9837-4 (hardcover) • ISBN 978-0-8027-9838-1 (reinforced)
[1. Animals—Fiction. 2. Comedy—Fiction. 3. Humorous stories.] I. Title.
PZ7.O526An 2010   [E]—dc22   2009018188

The art for this book was created using 140-lb Arches watercolor
paper, Higgins waterproof black ink, and assorted pen nibs.
The art was scanned and PhotoShop was used to place color.
Typeset in Bodoni Seventy Two
Book design by Donna Mark

Printed in China by C & C Offset Printing Co. Ltd., Shenzhen, Guangdong
2 4 6 8 10 9 7 5 3 1 (hardcover)
2 4 6 8 10 9 7 5 3 1 (reinforced)

All papers used by Walker & Company are natural, recyclable products
made from wood grown in well-managed forests. The manufacturing processes
conform to the environmental regulations of the country of origin.

Hen loved to tell jokes. Jokes like:

Why did the chicken go to the library?
To check out a *bawk, bawk, bawk*.

And:

How do comedians like their eggs?
Funny-side up!

Hen dreamed of standing on a stage in a comedy club and cracking up the crowd. She simply *had* to be a comedi-hen.

The farmer wanted her to lay eggs. But Hen was just too tired of working for chicken feed. Being an egg layer wasn't all it was cracked up to be.

"So you won't lay eggs, huh?" asked the farmer, using fowl language. "Well, come this Fry-day, you'll make a fine chicken dinner."

That night Hen talked to the other chickens.

"Where do chickens have the most feathers?" asked Hen.

"I don't know," said a chicken.

"On the outside!" she said. "And I plan on keeping it that way!"

So that night Hen flew the coop and headed across the field.

Early the next morning Hen saw a dog chasing its own tail.

"What are you doing, Dog?" she asked.

"I'm trying to make ends meet," he said.

"Would you please tell me your sad tale?" asked Hen.

"My sad tail can't talk, but I can tell you my story," said Dog.

"One night I was doing a comedy show for the sheep, and a wolf stole a side of beef from the smokehouse.

"'Doggone it, Dog, you're all bark and no bite,' the farmer said. He was so mad, I figured I better hightail it out of there!"

Hen told Dog about her dream to open a comedy club and asked him to join her.

Dog wagged his tail.

Why do dogs wag their tails?

Because no one will do it for them.

Dog and Hen were walking down the dusty road when they passed an old shed. A fat cat was lying on a wall. Mice were jumping all around him.

"You don't see that every day," said Hen. "Clearly that cat isn't any good at claw enforcement."

"So, Cat, can you 'hiss and tell' your story to us?" asked Dog.

"I want to be a performer. But my master didn't like my *cat*-erwauling."

"I sing funny songs, like 'Have Yourself a Furry Little Christmas' and 'Silent Mice.' The farmer told me he'd throw me in the river, so I left."

Hen and Dog told the cat about their idea for a comedy nightclub. It didn't take much *purrr*-suasion to get the cat to go with them.

Several hours later the three comedians came to a pasture. Standing outside the fence was a cow.

"You look udderly miserable," said Dog.

"If that cow were a musical note, she'd be a Beef-flat," Cat said to Hen.

"We herd there was a problem," said Hen. "No use crying over spilled milk. Let's see if we can help you fix it."

"I'm in a real stew. Last night the farmer said he was going to sell me to the butcher," said Cow. "See, I completely forgot about making milk. All I do is think about jokes. I guess you'd say I have Milk of Amnesia. So I snuck out of the barn, and now I'm *cow*-culating what my next *moo*ve should be."

Hen, Dog, and Cat told her of their plan for a comedy nightclub and invited her to join them. Cow said yes and rang her bell.

The four comedians walked and walked. They were getting tired and hungry. Finally, they passed an old house and looked inside. Sitting in the kitchen were three robbers. The leader said, "Don't eat all the food right now. We'll be hungry when we get back from robbing the bank."

The four comedians hid in the bushes and watched the robbers leave. As quickly as they could, they ran into the house and ate every last bit of food they could find.

"What did the mother ghost tell the baby ghost when he ate too fast?" asked Dog.

"Stop goblin your food," said Hen.

"Why did the student eat his homework?" asked Cat.

"The teacher told him it was a piece of cake," said Cow.

Tired and happy, the four comedians lay down and fell asleep.

Around midnight the robbers returned to the house. When the first robber stepped inside, he tripped on Cow. The second robber tripped on the first, and the third robber tripped on the second.

The four comedians awoke with a start. They did the only thing they could think of . . .

They told jokes.

Cow asked, "Why does a milking stool
have only three legs?
"Because the cow has the udder."
But the robbers just saw two horns and
heard . . .

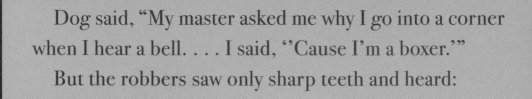

Dog said, "My master asked me why I go into a corner when I hear a bell. . . . I said, ''Cause I'm a boxer.'"
But the robbers saw only sharp teeth and heard:

Cat sang, "Over the counter and into my mouth, the tasty mouse will go!"
But the robbers felt only sharp claws and heard:

Meeeeooooowwwww!

And, of course, Chicken woke up and said:
"The farmer I worked for was so dumb, he plowed his field with a steamroller because he wanted mashed potatoes."
The robbers just felt her sharp beak and heard:

The robbers got so scared they
ran off and never came back.

Now the four comedians have a comedy club.
It's called COW-DOG KIT-HEN.
Animals come from far and wide.
The comedians do two shows a night.
And just like Hen dreamed . . .
They crack them up.